St. Helens Libraries

Please return / renew this item by the last date shown. Items may be renewed by phone and internet.

Telephone: **(01744) 676954 or 677822**
Email: **libraries@sthelens.gov.uk**
Online: **sthelens.gov.uk/librarycatalogue**

1 9 AUG 2022

For Keira and Jack

First published in 2022 in Great Britain by
Barrington Stoke Ltd
18 Walker Street, Edinburgh, EH3 7LP

www.barringtonstoke.co.uk

Text © 2022 Vashti Hardy
Illustrations © 2022 Natalie Smillie

The moral right of Vashti Hardy and Natalie Smillie to be
identified as the author and illustrator of this work has been
asserted in accordance with the Copyright, Designs and
Patents Act, 1988

A CIP catalogue record for this book is available
from the British Library upon request

ISBN: 978-1-80090-048-6

Printed by Hussar Books, Poland

CONTENTS

1

Mission Ready

Wardens Grace Griffin and Tom Eely stood opposite each other in the map room of Griffin House. Tom was a new recruit and they were checking they had all the tools and equipment they needed for their next mission.

"Stun stick?" asked Grace.

"Check," said Tom, and patted the bottom leg pocket of his brown warden's jumpsuit.

"Multi-tool?"

"Check." Tom pulled it from the thigh pocket of his right leg.

"Fingerprint dust?" Grace said.

"Check," Tom replied.

"Magnifier?"

"Check."

"Jelly babies?"

"Always," Tom said, grinning.

Grace laughed.

Then Grace saw that Tom looked relaxed, so with lightning speed she swept her leg beneath him. Tom reacted fast and leapt out of the way, then gave a lunge and arm strike.

Grace dodged the counter-attack, smiling. Tom had picked up the art of combat quickly since moving into Griffin House, and they'd had many weeks of fun as they trained together. It was great for Grace to have someone of her own age around.

"Combat rule number one: always be ready," said Grace. "I taught you well."

Watson the robot raven flew down from the mantelpiece and wing-chopped the back of Tom's knee.

Tom almost fell over, but he corrected his balance and turned around.

Watson flapped his mechanical wings so that he hovered in front of Tom. "Combat rule number two: look around for more than one attacker," Watson said.

Tom planted his feet firmly and extended his arms, facing Grace and Watson. "Combat rule number three: hold your nerve," Tom said firmly.

Faster than a flash, Grace whipped out her stun stick and twirled it between her fingers like an acrobat. "Even when faced with a stun stick," she said.

Grace pressed the small button to activate the stun stick and it emitted a silver light. Tom plunged his hand into his pocket to bring out his own stun stick, and with a burst of light their weapons locked as they began to lunge and block each other.

Grace's mum was standing next to the Griffin map. She now glanced up and said, "Well, you've come on superbly with your training, Tom."

The Griffin family were wardens of the Griffin map, an amazing invention that allowed them to teleport across the whole of Moreland from the city of Copperport where they lived. Great Grandma Griffin had created the map years ago. She'd wanted to find a way to travel to even the most remote places in Moreland when people needed help or there was a mystery to solve.

Until recently, Grace, her mum and her older brother, Bren, had been the only map wardens – keeping it in the family. But on a mission a few months ago, Grace had met Tom Eely, who had grown up in an orphanage on Eely Isle.

The orphanage had been run by a creative woman who had shared her love of designing new gadgets with Tom. But after she'd passed away, Tom was left alone on the remote island – until Grace turned up. Grace realised Tom's incredible talent for inventing would make him a great warden, and so she had convinced Mum to welcome him into the Griffin family.

It was wonderful to hear Mum praise Tom's progress after weeks of training. Grace grinned. She and Tom were looking forward to putting their skills into action by going on a mission, just the two of them. They were more than ready to find some crooks and solve big crimes. She'd been hoping Mum would notice it was time.

"Then we're ready for our own red mission," Grace said. She tried to make it sound like a fact rather than a question.

The Griffin map showed the entire country of Moreland. The many towns and villages each had their own gate on the map. The gates were portals, letting the wardens teleport into the map. The wardens answered calls for assistance and helped to ensure life in Moreland ran smoothly. If a gate flashed red, it was an emergency call, while a flashing blue gate meant it was a smaller problem.

Before Mum could answer Grace, Bren teleported into the room beside the map. He had left a short while ago to answer a call in the village of Brook Hollow.

"That was a short mission," said Mum.

"I'm not finished," Bren said. "I left my notebook here, so I've just come back to get it. I have a feeling this mission is going to need a lot of notes."

"It's hard to carry out a mission without the right equipment," Grace said, feeling smug at her brother's mistake. "Mission rule three: keep notes on the situation. *My* notebook is always in my pocket."

Bren glared at her.

"What's the problem in Brook Hollow?" asked Mum. "I don't think we've ever had a call from there before."

"Ravens," Bren replied.

"Ravens?" Watson squawked, and flew to land on the map table beside Bren. He ruffled his feathers.

Bren nodded. "Ravens have been attacking local residents. But like I say, I didn't get far because I needed my notebook."

A red gate started flashing on the map on the far side of the mountains – this was an emergency. Grace widened her eyes and glanced at Tom. This was their chance. She

looked hopefully at Mum, who wavered for a moment. Grace thought that even if Mum insisted on going with them, at least it would be an exciting mission.

"All right—" Mum started.

"Yes!" Grace interrupted, hurrying to the map. "Come on, Tom!" She grabbed a re-compass, which was a pocket-sized device they needed to teleport back home, and reached for the gate.

"Hey, not so fast!" said Mum.

Grace stopped. What had she forgotten? She hurried to pick up a pen to write down the name of the town where the gate flashed on a notepad beside the map. Leaving a note of your destination was teleporting rule number one. "Silly me," Grace said.

"No, Grace. I was about to say that you and Tom can go on a mission alone, but not this one.

You can take over the raven problem in Brook Hollow. Bren and I will answer the red call. Watson, you'd better go with them."

Grace sighed. "We're not really alone if Watson is with us."

Watson's cogs whirred and he clacked his beak. "Charming," he said.

"Sorry, Watson," Grace said, "but you know what I mean."

"Watson goes with you to Brook Hollow, Grace. Or you don't go at all," Mum said as she grabbed a re-compass.

Grace nodded. She loved having Watson around, but he could nag a bit.

"Sometimes I can read your thoughts, Grace Griffin," said Watson with a cough.

Mum took Bren's hand and they reached for the red gate. With a whirl and a flash of blue, they both disappeared into the map.

Grace looked over at Tom. The excitement of an emergency mission had disappeared like air escaping from a popped balloon. "Sorry. It doesn't look like we'll be able to use many of our fun gadgets or combat skills. I don't think raven pests are going to cause us too many problems."

A grin spread on Tom's lips. "Well, it's still a mission just for us," he said. "At least we can have a bit of fun together."

Grace nodded and patted her shoulder. "Come on, Watson. I know you're not programmed for fun, but problem ravens should be your specialist subject!" She loved to tease Watson.

"And being cheeky is yours, Grace!" Watson replied.

Grace wrote on the notepad beside the map: *Grace, Tom and Watson – gone to Brook Hollow to solve a raven riddle.* Then she took Tom's hand and said, "Ready?"

He nodded and Grace reached towards the flashing blue gate.

2

Brook Hollow

As they travelled through the gate, they were surrounded by bright blue crackling light. It was as if their bodies were being pulled in many directions at once until they landed with a jolt. Grace was used to teleporting, but it still felt as if her body had been broken into a thousand parts, then suddenly drawn back together.

They were on the edge of a small village in a valley between mountains with snowy peaks. There couldn't have been more than twenty wooden houses, all with neatly painted shutters, and primroses in the window boxes.

The grass was thick and emerald green. Lush pine forests lined the edges and the western end of the valley. A river ran past the village, and there was what looked to be a dam where the mountains narrowed in the distance to the west. The village was very remote, and there didn't appear to be much in the way of technology – just the red call box that the villagers had used to call the wardens.

"Mission rule one: assess the immediate danger," said Tom, and he adjusted his feet to a prepared combat stance.

"Well, yes," said Grace. "Except we know what we're teleporting into, because Bren told us."

"Oh, yeah, I guess we do."

They laughed.

"And it doesn't exactly look dangerous here," said Grace. "This village is like one of those

14

perfect ones shown on the front of a box of shortbread."

"So, we move to mission rule two: look after the caller," said Tom.

"Hmm, I can't see anybody," Grace replied. "But Bren spoke to someone when he arrived, and they'll probably be back soon. Let's have a look about and see if anyone appears or if we can spot any of these troublesome ravens ... Oh, wait! Here's one!" Grace prodded Watson on her shoulder and then tickled the cog under his chin, which always made his wing flap.

"Very funny," said Watson dryly.

A door opened in a pretty wooden house not far away. "Ah, you're back!" a gentleman said. "Except you're different wardens." He walked towards them wearing a checked cap, while stroking his strawberry-blond beard.

Grace whipped out her notepad. "Hello. Grace Griffin and Tom Eely at your service. We've been assigned to your case."

"I'm Frans Goran, a local farmer." Frans seemed to notice Watson and suddenly lunged at him, flapping his hands. "Go on, away with you before I wring your troublesome neck!"

"I beg your pardon!" said Watson, rearing back.

Frans stopped and stared at Watson.

"This raven is perfectly harmless," said Grace. "He's a robot raven and he's with us."

A deep frown appeared on Frans's face. "A ro-what?"

"Robot. The intelligent sort ... well, Watson likes to think he is," Grace teased, looking down at Watson and winking.

"We don't have any of these strange robot things here," said Frans, glancing at Watson as if he wasn't to be trusted.

Tom stepped forward. "We hear you've been having a spot of bother with ravens."

"Yes, terrible trouble," Frans said, and nodded hard.

"In what way?" asked Tom, taking out his notebook.

"I was out in the field over there with Bessie, my cow, when a bunch of ravens—"

Watson coughed. "It's actually a *flock* of ravens."

Frans took off his cap and scratched his bald head. "Pardon?"

"The name for a group of ravens is a flock," Watson said. "Or an unkindness, or a treachery, or a murder – but never a bunch."

Grace threw Watson a look and he shrugged his wings. "What?" Watson asked. "Details matter."

"Yes, thank you, Watson," said Grace. "Do continue, Mr Goran."

"I was over there, milking Bessie – she's my best cow – when ravens flew down, took my milking bucket and made off with it!"

"That must have been very annoying," said Tom.

"I would've let it go," Frans said, "but it's happened every day for a week. Bessie won't let me milk her now because she's so scared."

Tom looked to Grace, who nodded at him to continue. "And have there been any other incidents?" he asked.

"Sylvie had a whole bunch ..." Frans began, but then glanced at Watson again. "I mean, she had a *flock* of ravens squawking at the tops of their voices and swooping at her this morning. She was only going for her daily stroll down the west path along the valley."

An elderly man came out of what appeared to be a grocery shop nearby. "Any luck getting rid of those ravens?" he called over.

"Not yet, Wilf," Frans said. "The young wardens are on the case."

Wilf looked at the sky with a worried glance, nodded and went back inside.

"Poor Wilf was attacked when he took the west path up the valley to pick flowers yesterday," said Frans. "And Maria who owns the fruit stall couldn't get any apples from the orchard further down the valley because the ravens dive-bombed her every time she came near the trees!"

"This does seem like peculiar behaviour," said Grace. "And how long has it been going on for?"

"Over a week now."

"Hmm." Grace thought for a minute. "Thank you, Mr Goran. I think we have enough information to get going on this raven mystery."

"We do?" asked Tom.

Grace nodded and strolled up the path leading away from the village. She beckoned Tom to follow.

3

Raven Mischief

"Shouldn't we interview more residents?" Tom asked Grace.

"I think we have a strong lead to follow already. All of the four incidents had something in common."

Tom frowned. "They did?"

Watson chimed in, "The farmer's field, the west path and the orchard."

"I don't get it," said Tom.

"Frans pointed in their direction when he spoke," Grace explained. "They're all up this west end of the valley, in about the same direction."

"Oh, of course. Wow, you're good at this." Tom scratched his head. "And why might that matter?"

"The ravens only bother people when they go into that area," Grace said. "Creatures might attack if they are protecting something. Their chicks, for example."

"But the ravens do sound oddly aggressive, even if they're protecting chicks," said Watson.

Grace nodded. "Perhaps."

They carried on along the path and past the farmer's field. A cow that they thought must be Bessie was hiding in her shelter and gave a nervous moo as they passed.

A young woman was hurrying up the path in their direction. She wore a large-brimmed straw hat and carried a basket looped on her arm. She kept looking nervously behind her.

The woman didn't seem to notice Grace, Tom and Watson until she was upon them. When she saw them, she yelped, tripped up and fell forward. Wood logs spilled out of her basket.

Grace and Tom rushed to help her up.

"I'm so sorry," Grace said. "We didn't mean to startle you."

"I need to get home," the woman said. "I don't want to stay out here any longer than I have to." She brushed the dirt from her white apron.

Tom picked up the wood and put it back in her basket. The woman suddenly noticed Watson and yelped again.

"It's all right," said Tom. "He's our friend – a good raven."

"I've never felt so unwanted," Watson said, blinking. "Well, not since you didn't want to bring me on this mission about half an hour ago."

Grace turned to the lady. "I'm Grace Griffin, this is Tom Eely and this is Watson, our ever-so-friendly robot raven. We're from Copperport and we're here to help you."

"My name is Alice Brown," the lady said, still looking at Watson with fear in her eyes.

"You're afraid of being attacked by the ravens too," said Grace. She nodded to Tom to indicate that he should take notes.

Alice shook her head. "No ... well, yes – that's why I'm wearing my biggest hat. They can try to get past this, but they'll have a job." Alice pointed to the large brim on her hat. Then she lowered her voice to a whisper. "But it's the other thing that's got me scared."

"Other thing?" Grace asked.

Alice lowered her voice even more, and they could barely hear her say, "The mountain witch."

Grace, Tom and Watson exchanged glances.

"Did you say 'mountain witch'?" asked Grace.

Alice looked backwards nervously. "You know, the one from the tales."

Grace shook her head.

"The witch that stalks the mountains in her haunted moving house," Alice explained. "Surely you know the tale? It ends with, 'Witchy woo is going to get you!'"

"No, I don't believe we have that story in Copperport," Grace said, and looked to Tom.

"I didn't hear that story on Eely Isle either," Tom said.

"Well, everyone in the mountains knows the story," Alice said. "And it's not just a story. It's real because I saw it. The witch's haunted house is in the forest. It appeared out of nowhere!"

They all looked towards the pine forest in the west.

"Ravens *and* a witch *and* a haunted house?" said Grace.

Alice nodded. "The witch can turn herself into a raven, and then she can control the whole flock. It says so in the stories. And she lives in a house that's so haunted it can move! I'm off to tell the villagers. Something needs to be done about her."

With that, Alice hurried away.

"There's no need to panic. Leave it to us. We're here to—" Grace started, but Alice was gone, running along the path back to the village.

"What do we do now?" Tom said, watching Alice hurrying away.

"These remote villages are always full of myths of monsters and witches and things," said Grace. "It sounds like the village is working itself into a tizzy about a few ravens, when they're probably just being protective of their chicks. And I'm guessing this house is an old woodcutter's hut they've forgotten about. It's time to prove to the people of Brook Hollow that there's nothing to be afraid of. Come on."

They carried on up the path past the apple orchard, towards the thick pine forest.

"I don't believe in witches," Tom said. "But what if this house in the forest *is* haunted?" He wiggled his fingers and made a ghostly "Wooo!" sound.

"Then we'll zap it with a stun stick," laughed Grace.

Watson tutted. "You two need to take this more seriously."

"Lighten up, Watson. There's no such thing as witches or ghosts," said Grace. "And monsters usually turn out to be people, and—"

Suddenly, Watson let out a squawk. "But there *are* real ravens!"

Caws filled the air as a hundred large black birds shot from the pine forest towards them.

4

Into the Forest

The wardens froze, baffled. There were so
many ravens! They swarmed the sky to the
west like a great incoming storm cloud.

"Maybe they're heading for the village,"
suggested Grace. But as she said the words, she
knew she was wrong. The ravens were zooming
down at an angle, right towards the spot where
she, Tom and Watson were standing.

"What do we do?" asked Tom, his voice high
and panicked.

"The orchard is too far back to reach for shelter," Grace said. "We could try to make the forest."

But the ravens were too fast.

Grace looked to Watson. She had an idea. "This is your moment, buddy."

"What do you mean?" Watson asked.

"Divert them," Grace said. "Fly up, make lots of noise and lead the ravens away to the north. Tom and I will run to the forest for cover and to check out this strange house."

Watson gave a quick nod and took flight. "I'll send out a sonic shock wave to confuse them too." His mechanical wings were fast, and after a few flaps he was soaring towards the flock.

Grace grabbed Tom's arm. "Run for the forest!"

They darted towards the trees. Before they reached them, Grace glanced back. Watson was banking left in the sky, a sonic pulse radiating from him in translucent air waves.

The ravens all hovered for a moment and began flapping in circles, not knowing where to go. Then Watson squawked at them and began leading them north.

Thanks to Grace and Tom's training, they were soon running between tree trunks in the safety of the forest.

They paused, hands on knees, to catch their breath. The forest floor was carpeted with fallen pine needles and cones. It smelt sweet and citrusy and of damp bark.

"Will Watson be all right?" asked Tom.

"He's fitted with the fastest wings in Moreland," Grace said. "He'll catch up with us soon."

"The ravens seemed really angry. What do you think we did to annoy them?"

Grace shrugged. "It seems they don't want us here. Let's find out why." She pulled her binoculars from a jumpsuit pocket and looked to the treetops.

"What are you doing?" Tom asked.

"Looking for nests. The ravens might be protecting chicks."

"Oh yes, good idea." Tom pulled out his binoculars to do the same. "You're rather excellent at this."

"At what?"

"Being a warden," Tom said. "You always seem to know what to do."

Grace smiled. "You're doing pretty good too."

"Really? The training is all very well, but out here it feels different. My heart is still pounding from that raven attack, but you're as cool as a breeze!"

It was a welcome change to be on a mission with Tom. Grace had been so used to being the youngest in the family and looking up to Bren and Mum, and now someone looked up to her. It felt good.

Tom looked around the forest. "The haunted house must be here somewhere."

"Hey, if it is haunted, we could become ghost hunters as well as wardens!" Grace joked.

"We'd need to invent more equipment," said Tom. "Ghost trappers and zappers and the like." He looked thrilled by the idea – there was nothing Tom loved more than inventing new gadgets.

"Hey, look." Grace pointed into the gloom. "Can you see that dark shape? That could be a building – a woodshed or a haunted house! Come on, let's go and see."

They trudged past the ferns into the deepening gloom, and Grace became aware of how silent it was. There didn't seem to be any animals or birds around. Tom looked about with a frown and had become quiet too.

The pine trees opened out into a small clearing with a peculiar house in the middle.

"That's no woodshed," said Grace.

5

The Haunted House

The house was made of a mass of different styles, with all manner of materials patched together. The roof was thatched, like a cottage, with a metal chimney poking through the middle. The walls were mostly wooden planks, but there were metal patches in places.

It was the windows that drew Grace's eye the most because they appeared to be in the shape of cogs. A beam of sunlight had fought its way between the treetops and shone on a copper cog-shaped front door. Three silver steps led up to it. There was no knocker or bell, and no house name.

"How cool is that door?" said Grace. "We should get one like that for Griffin House."

"It's the strangest house I've ever seen," said Tom.

"Hello?" called Grace. "Is anybody at home?" She climbed the steps and knocked on the door. There was no answer.

"Hello?" Grace knocked more firmly. The door creaked open a few centimetres.

Tom and Grace shrugged at each other.

Grace called into the gap in the doorway, "We're wardens of the Griffin map from Copperport here to investigate why ravens are attacking the people of Brook Hollow. Perhaps we could have a quick word? Maybe you've seen them too, or they might have attacked here?"

The wind whistled through the trees, and the light vanished from above as a dark cloud passed over. Tom took a step closer to Grace.

She glanced at him. "Are you all right, Tom? You've turned a bit pale."

"It's this place," Tom replied. "I know we were joking, but it's actually pretty spooky. Did you see how the sunlight disappeared from above after you knocked? Doesn't that seem a bit ... scary?"

Grace thought for a moment. She didn't get scared easily, but she had to admit the atmosphere was eerie here. She drew back her shoulders. "That was just a coincidence. On a practical note, the door to this house *is* open, and we didn't force it, so there could be someone injured inside who needs our help. Come on, we're going in."

"I don't know, Grace," Tom said. "Maybe we should wait or go back to the village."

"Come on," Grace urged. "Wardens have no time to hesitate. Not if someone could be in danger."

She pushed the door, which swung open, creaking loudly.

Inside was as strange as the outside. There was a large main room which looked to be a kitchen, dining and living room in one. A couple of doors at the back led to what Grace presumed must be a bedroom and bathroom. There were many cupboards and shelves around the edges of the main room, plus a kitchen sink, a stove, a single armchair with a knitted cover and a small table with one dining chair. The shelves were jam-packed with various tools and bits of machinery.

Grace took a few steps further inside and called out again. "Hello? Is anyone at home?"

The floorboards and walls creaked noisily.

"What was that?" asked Tom.

"Just the wind," Grace said.

The front door banged behind them, and Tom leapt in the air.

"What in Moreland has got into you?" said Watson, flying through the door. He landed on Grace's shoulder.

Tom put a hand on his heart. "Oh, it's only you. I thought it was a ghost!"

"Look, the stove is hot," said Grace, feeling warmth radiating from it. "Someone must have been here recently."

The building made another eerie creak. Tom grabbed Grace's arm. "I don't like this at all!"

"There will be a perfectly rational explanation," Grace said. "The wind has picked up, or the house foundations might be a bit unstable, or something like that."

Grace continued to look around the house. There were so many curious things in here, she couldn't help but touch them as she passed. Her attention was caught by a metal bird almost as tall as Grace that had a wind-up mechanism at its back between its wings. Grace lifted one of the wings and a window to a clockwork motor became visible. "Look at this huge mechanical bird, Tom!" she said.

But before he could answer, the walls gave a groan and the floor rattled beneath their feet, making Grace judder. Tom yelped and darted for the door.

Grace called after him, "It's just the wind!"

"I think that's called losing your nerve," said Watson.

"Come on, we'd better go after him," Grace said. "Tom!" she called into the forest. "It's just the wind – don't worry."

The forest gloom made it difficult to see which way he had gone.

"Look," said Watson, pointing his wing to some scuffs in the forest floor. "He went that way."

They found Tom not far away, with his back to a tree, catching his breath.

"Are you all right?" Grace asked. "The creaking back there was just the wind, or dodgy foundations. Honestly, I'm sure there's nothing to worry about."

She put her arm around him.

"I feel like an idiot," Tom said miserably.

"Come on, we can go back and prove it's just a creaky old house," Grace said. But she noticed Tom's eyes were pooling with tears. "Or we could just go back to the village if you want?"

"I'm not upset because you want to go back," Tom said. "I know I was silly to get scared then, and that it's probably just a creaky old house. But I let you down. I ran off without you, and that isn't what wardens do. You always seem to know the right thing to do, Grace, but I haven't got a clue. Maybe I was alone on Eely Isle for too long and I forgot how to look out for anyone other than myself. I'm a total failure."

Grace's heart twisted at his words. She knew he wasn't giving himself a chance. "Look, Tom. We've barely even started to investigate this mystery. Remember what I told you about my first proper mission? So much went wrong, and most of it was my fault. But I learned and I got through it, and I was stronger afterwards.

You need to stop worrying about letting me down."

"I hate to admit Grace is right, but she totally is," said Watson, flying to land on Tom's shoulder. "Let's go back to the house and investigate properly. Wardens don't run – we solve things by working together and getting to the bottom of what's going on."

6

The Wrong Lever

Tom wiped his eyes with his sleeve and nodded. Then they walked back towards the peculiar house.

"Look," said Grace, pointing to the bottom of the house. She knelt on the ground and peered under the house. "See how it's raised above the ground a little? It's propped up by these thick stilts at the corners. No wonder the wind gets underneath and makes it creak."

"Maybe it's raised like that to keep the damp out," said Tom.

"Excellent. See, you are thinking like a warden now," said Grace. "When you start to look at the situation more closely, you can see the answers. And look at the walls and shutters." She pointed to one of the windows. "They look like they're held together by all sorts of screws and fixings. No doubt a strong gust of wind would shake the walls a bit."

"Look at the roof!" said Tom.

At first Grace had thought the roof was thatched, but now she realised that it was covered with twigs not straw. "Ravens' nests!"

"Well, at least we know where the ravens are coming from," Watson said. The cogs in his head whirred. He flew up and circled the house. "I can't see any chicks."

"Now that I think about it, it's probably a bit late in the season for ravens to lay eggs," said Tom. "There were a lot of birds back on Eely Isle, so I know a bit about them," he explained to Grace.

"So protecting chicks can't be the reason why they're so cross," Grace said. "Let's go back into the house and check all the rooms."

They walked back up the creaky steps to the door.

Inside the house, they all looked more closely around the main room. They peered inside cupboards and found lots of machinery parts. The only furniture in the bedroom was one neatly made bed.

"What about this cupboard?" said Tom, pointing to a door in the main room that Grace hadn't noticed.

"Check inside," Grace called. She had noticed a large lever sticking out of the floor and was kneeling to examine it.

Watson waddled along the floor nearby. "Perhaps you should just make notes and not mess with things," he said to Grace.

"Stop being a spoilsport, Watson. How can we possibly solve a mystery without taking a few risks?"

"I don't know, Grace, but caution has its place."

Grace leaned on the lever and was about to tell Watson to stop being dramatic when it suddenly gave way beneath her.

"Oops," said Grace.

Flapping his wings, Watson said, "See?"

Grace tried to pull the lever back up, but it was stuck. "Never mind," she said. "It's probably something to do with the plumbing. I'm sure it's fine."

"This cupboard has some strange wheels in it," called Tom.

A loud thud echoed through the house.

"What was that?" Tom asked.

A loud whirring came from beneath the floorboards. Teaspoons rattled on the table. Everything began shaking.

With a lurch, Grace, Tom and Watson were thrown to the floor.

"What's happening?" said Grace.

The floor tilted, then levelled, then tilted again.

"What did you do?" said Watson.

"Nothing! The house is doing this itself," said Grace.

"Look out of the window," said Tom. "The trees are moving!"

Grace's heart thumped against her ribs. "It's not the trees; it's us! Quick, we need to get out!"

They bolted for the door. By the time
they reached the steps, the whole house was
hovering a couple of metres from the ground.

"Jump!" said Grace, taking Tom's hand.

They landed with a thud, rolling over leaves and mud.

"How can a house float?" Tom said. "What's going on?"

Creaks, clunks and judders filled the air as the house continued to rise.

Tubes grew from two metal feet underneath the house, many rings dropping from inside, stacking and building, pushing the house higher and higher.

"Are those legs?" Grace said.

The house wobbled and groaned. It took a step towards them.

"Argh!" Grace and Tom darted back.

"Stop the house, Grace!" called Watson.

To make things worse, squawks filled the air above. The flock of ravens spiralled above, then dived towards them.

"Not the ravens too!" said Tom.

"Run!" shouted Grace. She didn't want to keep running away, but she didn't think they had much choice.

They began leaping over tree stumps and fallen branches, but they hadn't got far when a voice shouted, "Wretched children!"

Grace and Tom skidded to a stop. In front of them was a very wrinkly, very fierce-looking old lady. She wore a cloak and green hat and was brandishing a stick.

Three words shot into Grace's head.

The mountain witch.

7

The Mountain Witch

"What have you done to my house?" yelled the old woman. She barged between Grace and Tom.

"We're sorry, we were trying—" Grace started to say, but the old woman ran towards the house. The ravens spiralled above, cawing angrily.

Grace watched the old woman reach the house and hook her stick onto the rising steps. She flicked something and a ladder dropped.

"Come on, we'd better help," said Grace. She felt scared, but she knew her fears were a bit daft – this woman probably wasn't a witch. Grace had to be strong because if she panicked, so would Tom. Plus they had an out-of-control house to fix.

The old woman pulled herself up the ladder and onto the steps as the house tottered and swayed, then she hurried inside. Grace was about to attempt climbing the ladder herself when a loud hiss sounded, then the house shuddered and stopped moving.

The house began sinking, its legs folding in on themselves until it was almost back on the ground. The ravens stopped cawing and began landing on the roof.

The old woman reappeared on the front steps. "What in all the mountains of Moreland did you think you were doing messing around in my house? Can't I be left alone in peace for just one day?"

"We're sorry," said Grace.

"Honestly – trespassing, tampering, snooping!" the old woman went on.

"We didn't mean to cause trouble or to set off ... well, whatever that was that happened to your house," Grace said. "We're wardens of the Griffin map from Copperport. We received a call about ravens attacking the villagers of Brook Hollow for no reason, and we're here to investigate."

The old woman cackled with laughter. "Attacking for no reason, eh?"

"Well, none that we've managed to figure out yet," Grace said.

"You're wardens, you say?" the old woman asked. "Never heard of the likes. Sounds like you're mischief-makers to me."

"Honestly, we're not," said Tom. "We just want to stop the ravens attacking people."

Hundreds of black raven eyes stared at them suspiciously from the roof.

"Well, I'll likely be moving off again soon," the old woman went on. "The ravens will follow me, so the villagers won't have to put up with them for long." She sat down heavily on the step.

"But don't you live here?" asked Grace.

"Here, there, everywhere." The old woman started searching her pockets.

Grace noticed she looked hot after all the effort of rescuing the house. "Here," said Grace, passing her a hankie.

The old woman wiped her brow.

"You're very active for ..." Grace stopped herself.

"Say it. For an old lady?" The woman laughed.

Watson flew to land on Grace's shoulder and whispered, "It's rude to be ageist."

"Well, well!" The old woman's glassy blue eyes lit up at the sight of Watson. "What have we here?"

"This is Watson, a robot raven," said Grace. "Robots are mechanical animals which—"

"I know what robots are," the old woman interrupted.

"Really?" said Tom. "The villagers of Brook Hollow hadn't come across such a thing before."

"Well now, they wouldn't, would they?" The old woman tutted.

"What exactly just happened with your house?" asked Grace. "It seemed to be elevating and trying to ... walk?"

"That's right," the old woman said. "It's full of cogs, pistons and all sorts of mechanics. The corners have extra-thick walls that hide the extending legs. It can go as high as the treetops and I can steer it from place to place. That way I can travel wherever I like and stay away from pesky people like you. There's even a hidden hatch so I can pull heavy things up through the floor instead of using the steps."

"Amazing!" said Grace and Tom together.

"You're definitely not a mountain witch like they say, are you?" said Grace.

The old woman laughed. "No, I'm Nellie Grey, this is my clockwork house and these ravens are my friends. My only friends," she said, sounding sad.

"Oh, I'm sorry," said Tom.

Nellie shrugged. "I'm used to it. I've not had human friends since I was a girl."

"Really?" said Grace. She thought Nellie seemed nice and rather interesting now that everything had calmed down. "Why ever not?"

Nellie paused and looked between Grace and Tom. Instead of answering, she said, "Now, are you two going to tell me your names and go inside and make me a nice cup of tea or what? I think you owe it to me after causing such trouble. Then we can talk."

"I'm Grace Griffin and this is Tom Eely, and we'd best make you that tea then."

Grace hurried inside with Tom. They found the kettle, put it on the stove and made a pot of tea.

Then they all sat together on the steps. Grace passed Nellie a mug and she took a big gulp.

"Now I'm going to tell you my real story," she said, and reached into her inside jacket pocket.

8

Nellie's Story

Nellie pulled a small metal bird from her pocket.

"Is that a robin?" asked Tom.

"It is," Nellie replied. "I can see you know your birds, young man. This is the first thing I made as a child." She wound a pin in the robin's side and let go. Its little beak opened and it began chirping. Then its small wings extended and it flew upwards, flying in small circles in the clearing.

"That's brilliant!" said Tom.

"I made it when I was six," said Nellie
proudly. "My parents made clocks in our
mountain village, so I grew up around cogs and
springs. They let me play with all the tools
and this was what I made first. Want to see
another?"

"Yes, please!" said Grace and Tom together.

Nellie went inside, then came back out
pushing the large silver bird Grace had seen
earlier. "I added wheels to the feet when I

couldn't carry her any more," Nellie explained. "She's not as advanced as your robot raven, but she's pretty sturdy and can carry a good weight. I used to fly around on her when I was younger. All the controls are still in working order. Wind up here and you're off!"

"Brilliant!" said Tom, grinning.

Grace wanted to see more of Nellie's inventions, but then she remembered that they were actually on an investigation. She needed to get to the bottom of why the ravens were attacking the villagers.

"So the ravens are your friends?" Grace asked.

Nellie nodded. "I always loved to feed them. At first it was just a few, then the colony grew."

"And they follow you wherever you go?"

"Since I was young," Nellie replied.

"So you must have an idea why they are attacking the villagers?"

With a sigh, Nellie said, "It all started years ago. People in my home village were wary of my mechanical birds. They thought I was using some dark magic to bring them to life."

"Really?" asked Grace.

"These mountain parts are remote, as you know," Nellie said. "People don't get to see all the fancy inventions in the cities and towns of Moreland, and they don't have much interest in learning about technology. They'd rather believe in witches and dark magic."

"So the people of your village thought you were strange?" Grace said.

"Parents wouldn't let their children play with me when I was younger. And I was a shy child – I didn't speak much. So when they asked me about the magic, I just shrugged. Soon they were calling me the wacky witch, which seems to have followed me even now."

"Why did you leave your village?" asked Tom.

"My parents were killed in a rockfall not far from home when I was fifteen. People in the village started to say it was my magic that caused it, so I left."

"How horrible," said Grace.

"I ran away into the mountains to start my own life and began building this clockwork house. I decided if I wasn't welcome in the villages, I would make the mountains my home and move around from place to place. That way I could get on with doing what I loved and no one could hurt me again."

Grace's heart twisted for Nellie. She must have been so upset to have lost her parents and her home. Grace looked across to Tom and gave him a sad smile. Tom had suffered the loss of his orphanage home and family in the past.

"I had an idea of going to the city once, of creating a clockwork toy shop," Nellie went on. "But the longer I stayed out in the mountains, the harder it seemed to try that. Sometimes I'd go into villages to try to trade for supplies, but everyone knew of me as the mountain witch, so I never stayed long. It's the same today."

"And the ravens follow you wherever you go?" asked Grace.

"Yes, they come everywhere with me and my house. They're very loyal and protective of people being unkind to me."

"Oh, I see," said Grace. "They're protecting *you*."

One raven flew from the roof and landed on Nellie's arm. It looked at Grace and Tom with some suspicion.

"It's all right – they mean us no harm," said Nellie. She turned to Grace again. "The ravens have become a bit over-enthusiastic in their protection of me lately. It's hard to stop them! I'll keep an eye on them, and we'll be on our way again soon."

"Well, at least we can get the mission finished," Grace said. "We'll go back to the village and explain. Everything will be fine." She hopped to her feet.

"Thank you," said Nellie. "It's the first kindness anyone has shown me in a long time."

"Perhaps you'll find some more in the next place you stop," Tom said, smiling.

"I hope you do too. Good luck," said Grace, waving goodbye.

9

Tom Steps Up

Clouds dotted the sky as they walked back towards Brook Hollow. Grace didn't think it would take long to explain the misunderstanding to the villagers. She would tell them there was no mountain witch and reassure them that the ravens would keep away and move along soon.

"I'll call Mum and update her as we walk," said Grace. She took out her digi-com, a piece of technology her mum had invented so the Griffins could contact each other wherever they were in Moreland. Grace pressed the neon yellow circle in the middle of the palm-sized white disc. "Mum, are you there?"

"Grace, I can't talk now," Mum replied. "A huge storm has blown into the north and calls are coming in thick and fast. Are you all right?" The line crackled.

"We're fine. We've got to the bottom of the raven riddle – it was—"

"Grace, the signal is breaking up. I didn't catch that. It must be the storm scrambling the waves."

"Mum, I said we've—" Grace started to say.

"What's that, Grace? I didn't hear a word. Look, you sound fine. The storm is heading east, so it shouldn't affect your area. I've got to go. A tree's fallen on a house and—"

The line crackled again, then went quiet.

"I guess your mum and Bren still have their hands full," said Tom.

"It might be raining where Mum is, but it looks fine here," said Grace with a shrug.

As they carried on along the path, they noticed the villagers had gathered in a field. Frans Goran, the farmer, was standing on a wooden crate before the villagers, giving a speech. They seemed quite angry and worked up, waving their hands and pointing their fingers towards the forest.

"Looks like they're having a village meeting," said Grace. "I'd better explain what's been happening before things get out of hand." She headed for Frans.

"Alice Brown has confirmed to us that the mountain witch has come to our valley," Frans was saying. "We should've realised she was sending those ravens to try to bewitch us! Well, enough is enough. The mountain witch needs to know she's not welcome here."

Frans banged the pitchfork he was holding on the crate. "I say we march down together and drive the witch and her ravens away."

Grace stepped in front of him. "Everybody, calm down," she said. "There will be no need to drive anyone away. We've spoken to the woman you're calling a witch, and she's a harmless old lady."

"Tell that to my poor Bessie." Frans scowled, and the villagers nodded.

Grace looked Frans square in the eye, because Mum always said that was a good way to let people know you mean what you say. "She's actually a really nice lady and very inventive," Grace said. "If you'd just listen for a moment."

But Frans looked away and said, "It's time to take matters into our own hands." The rest of the villagers called out in agreement.

The elderly man, Wilf, stepped up beside Grace. "I'm not sure why Frans called you to help in the first place. You come from the city. What do you know of the mountains and what lies here?"

"But—" Grace tried to say.

"We've decided we've had enough," Frans said. "We need to take action against the witch!" He jumped off the crate.

Watson whispered into Grace's ear from her shoulder, "They've clearly worked themselves into a frenzy. We need to think of a Plan B before they storm into the forest."

But Grace was out of ideas. She couldn't use martial arts or stun sticks to help her now. What could she do when people wouldn't listen?

Then she felt a hand on her arm, and Tom stepped up onto the crate.

He cleared his throat and said, "Excuse me, everyone."

"What's he doing?" Grace whispered to Watson, who shrugged his wings.

"Excuse me!" Tom said again, forcefully so that the villagers turned and looked to him.

"What is it, lad?" asked Frans.

"I don't come from the city," Tom said. "I'm originally from a remote island called Eely Isle. I lived there by myself for a long time. I know what it's like to be alone and afraid." Tom took a long breath.

"Go on, boy," said Frans.

"People can be scared of the unknown. I was wary of all outsiders. I thought they wished me harm. Then Grace Griffin came to Eely Isle and found me." Tom looked down at Grace and smiled. "She showed me that the things you're scared of aren't always dangerous. Just because someone is a stranger, it doesn't mean that they should be feared."

Pride swelled in Grace's chest. Tom had the villagers' attention. All eyes were on him.

"Please give the old lady of the forest a chance," said Tom. "Her name is Nellie Grey. We can bring her to the village so that she can meet you and tell you her story, just as she did to us. Then you'll see there's nothing to be afraid of." Tom glanced at Grace, who nodded in agreement. If the villagers could stay calm enough to meet Nellie, they would realise that their mountain-witch story was ridiculous.

The villagers exchanged glances. Frans nodded thoughtfully.

"It's working," whispered Watson.

Then Alice Brown suddenly pointed to the sky. "What's that over there?"

Everyone looked to the west, where Alice was pointing. Something thick and dark was on the horizon.

10

The Storm

"Is it more ravens?" asked Frans, looking at the dark patch in the distance.

"Of course not. It's just a storm cloud," said Grace. She lowered her voice and turned to Tom and Watson. "A rather big, fierce-looking storm cloud, moving in fast. Perhaps the storm Mum and Bren are dealing with further north is spreading our way."

A drop of rain splashed on Grace's cheek. Then another.

"That came out of nowhere," said Alice.

"Storms don't usually arrive so fast," said Frans.

Grace's digi-com went off in her pocket. She pulled it out and pressed the button. "Mum, is that you?"

"Grace, the lines are still bad, but ... warn you ... changed direction. Flood water from the north is heading ..."

"Mum, you're breaking up. What's wrong?"

"Danger ... the dam ... flood on way ... could burst."

"Mum?" Grace said.

The digi-com crackled, then fell silent.

At first Grace didn't understand Mum's warning, but then she remembered the dam they had seen further upriver when they had first landed in Brook Hollow. Was that what Mum was talking about?

Everyone in the field had fallen silent too. They were all looking at Grace.

At the western end of the valley beyond the forest, rain fell in great sheets from the dark clouds.

"It's the mountain witch. She's tricked us," called one of the villagers.

Grace put a hand up. "It's a storm. Stay calm. Nobody has caused it – it's nature."

But the dark clouds had reached them now, and heavy drops of rain bombarded them. People began running back to the village, shouting, "The witch has cursed us!"

"Stop!" Grace called. "The dam is at risk of breaking. You must listen!"

But no one was listening. Besides, the fierce pelting of the rain drowned out Grace's shouts.

"Grace, if what we heard is right and the dam breaks, then we need to get everyone to safety, and fast," said Watson.

"Agreed," Grace said. "We should tell everybody to head up to the high ground at the edge of the valley. I'll go after the villagers. Watson, you go with Tom to tell Nellie. Sit on his shoulder – you can't fly in this." Grace's hair and warden uniform were already soaked.

But as she moved to run, an earth-shattering crack echoed through the valley.

Grace froze. "Oh no. I think that was the dam!"

Quick as a flash, Grace whipped her binoculars from her pocket and focused on the far end of the valley to take a closer look. She was right – a thick jet of water spouted from a crack in the dam.

"It's holding, but it could break at any moment," Grace said to Watson and Tom.

This was serious. It wouldn't take long for the flood to reach them if the dam collapsed completely. Did they even have time to get to higher ground? They had the re-compass and could teleport back to Copperport, but they couldn't abandon everyone else.

"I don't think we'll get everyone to high ground in time," Grace said. "What do we do?" Watson and Tom looked at her with wide panicked eyes.

Another large crack sounded. They had no time to dither. Then it came to her. "Nellie's clockwork house!" Grace said. "At full height, it should be above flood level. If we get everyone in the house before the dam breaks, we stand a chance!"

"Brilliant!" said Tom.

"We'll all go to Nellie's together. It'll be quickest," said Grace.

They ran for the forest.

Swiftly they explained to Nellie that the dam could burst at any moment. "I don't like how the villagers have behaved," Nellie said, "but no one deserves to be caught in a flood. Hurry inside. Let's put this house into action!"

Nellie released the large lever inside, then instructed Grace and Tom to open various cupboards and turn wheels and press different buttons. "Steady as she goes – level her up now," Nellie said.

Whirrs and thuds shuddered through the house. The pine trees outside began moving past as they rose up and up.

"Will the house be strong enough to stay up in a flood?" Grace asked.

"The legs have titanium cores," Nellie said. "This house has survived a fair few storms in her time. Watson, fly over there and pull down that hook, will you?"

Watson did as he was asked, and a tube extended from the ceiling.

"That's the periscope," Nellie explained. "You can be navigator, Grace. Your eyes are probably better than mine. And, Tom, you can help at the steering wheel. I usually manage it all on my own, but we need to move fast, so it'll be easier with three of us."

Grace pressed her eyes to the tube. The tops of the pine trees came into view, being hammered by driving rain.

"What about the ravens on your roof? They'll get soaked," said Tom.

"They'll have already flown themselves to safety on high ground," said Nellie. "Don't worry about them."

Nellie asked Tom to pull another lever. "Careful you get the right one – we don't want the trapdoor opening with Watson standing on it!"

The house was now at full height.

"Grasp the wheel, Tom. I'll control the speed and you can steer. Now, direct us through the trees to the village, Grace!"

11

The Dam

Some of the trees were tightly packed together,
so Grace had to think quickly to find the best
way forward. The relentless rain didn't make it
easy to see as Grace called to Tom to steer from
left to right.

Soon they hit the open area of the valley
and could pick up their pace. Huge puddles
flooded some areas already. Nellie wasn't afraid
of going fast, and Grace's stomach squeezed as
they splashed across the valley. The clockwork
house strode onwards, making great progress.

They were almost at the village when the loudest crack of all sounded.

Grace spun the periscope around. In the far distance, she saw that the dam had collapsed and a rush of water had broken through. Nellie

brought the house to a stop beside the village, and they all dashed over to the front door and looked down. The panicked villagers were clustered together, looking towards the dam end of the valley, not knowing what to do.

Nellie unhooked the ladder, and it clattered down towards the villagers.

"The dam has broken! Hurry up here!" called Grace.

"Hurry up!" called Nellie. "There's room for you all."

The villagers stared up at the mechanical house with a mixture of disbelief and concern on their faces.

"Watson, they're frozen in shock," Grace said. "We have to go down and convince them it's the only way to escape the flood. Tom, you help them get inside up here with Nellie."

Grace hurried down the ladder with Watson on her shoulder. "There's no time to get to higher ground!" she called. "Climb up into the clockwork house. Now! It will keep you safe, and it's the only chance you've got."

For a moment, nobody moved, then Alice Brown began climbing up the ladder. "She's right – there's no other way. Come on!"

The villagers hurried up into the house, one after the other. Tom helped them over the top step and inside.

"Where's Frans the farmer? I can't see him," said Grace.

"There!" shouted Watson. "He's gone to the field where his cow is."

"Oh no! Frans, come back!" Grace yelled, running towards the field. "We haven't got time."

"Grace!" Watson squawked on her shoulder. "The flood is coming!" The rain battered his body.

They caught up with Frans in the field.

"I'm not leaving my Bessie!" said Frans.

"I'm so sorry, but you don't have a choice, Frans," Grace said. She desperately wanted to help but couldn't think of a way to save Bessie.

All the villagers apart from Frans were now safely inside the house.

"There's no time!" Grace tugged at Frans's arm. Then she looked up to see the clockwork house striding towards them. It stopped above Bessie. Nellie opened the trapdoor in the floor and threw down a large chain and harness.

"Hook this around the cow and I'll hoist her up!" called Nellie.

Water rumbled in the distance.

"Hurry!" Tom yelled.

Grace, Watson and Frans swiftly wrapped
the harness around Bessie and signalled to
Nellie to pull her up. Then Grace pushed Frans

up the ladder ahead of her. The water crashed through the forest where the house had been that morning.

"I'll fly up – you climb," said Watson.

"Hurry, both of you – the flood water is almost here!" called Nellie.

When Grace reached the top of the ladder, she turned around to check on Watson. Where was he? She looked down to see the rain bombarding him and stopping his flight.

"Save yourself!" Watson cried.

"Watson, no!" Grace cried. She dropped down a couple of rungs on the ladder and reached for him. Using all her strength, she grabbed his wing and hurled him up towards the door.

Then the water hit her. It was like being slammed into a wall. Grace's hand was ripped from the ladder, and she was pulled away in the rush of waves.

"Grace!" Tom yelled.

By some miracle, as Grace fell she remembered to reach into her left bicep pocket and pull on the hidden loop. It activated the emergency life jacket that was built into her jumpsuit. Air rushed into the pocket – just enough to keep her afloat. But the clockwork house was growing smaller by the second as the rush of water pulled her along the valley.

She looked around frantically, hoping she could grab a treetop to stop herself from being carried further, but she was also terrified of crashing into something. Ice-cold water splashed and gurgled around her so she could hardly breathe. Her whole body felt as if it was being stabbed by a thousand freezing pins.

A treetop whizzed towards her and she reached out to grab it, but the branch snagged

her jumpsuit. The air hissed out of her life jacket. She was overwhelmed by panic.

"Grace! Stay afloat – I'm coming!"

Grace turned round to see a sight she couldn't believe. There was Tom, zooming towards her through the rain on Nellie's huge mechanical bird!

Grace kicked with all her strength to stay afloat. While he flew, Tom grabbed his emergency rope from his large thigh pocket, clipped it to his belt and threw the other end towards Grace. "Catch it!"

She lunged as the rope snaked towards her. As she grabbed the end, the mechanical bird lurched.

"I'm switching to hover mode," Tom explained. "Just hold on a bit longer, Grace."

The mechanical bird hovered, and Tom hauled Grace towards him by the rope. "I think the water is slowing. Just hold on."

"I'm not letting go for anything!" Grace called.

Tom was right – the water was easing as the flow calmed down at the other end of the valley.

"I think I can pull you back to the house now," he called.

The rain stopped, and the rush of flood lost its power. Tom flew back to the house, towing Grace through the receding water.

When they reached the house, Tom hovered by the ladder, making sure Grace had hold of the rungs, then he flew up and landed back on the steps. Grace pulled herself up the ladder, and the villagers helped her inside. Everyone fussed around her and wrapped her in towels.

Tom pushed past everyone and gave Grace a hug. "Thank goodness you're alive," Tom said.

"Thank you for saving me, Tom." Grace smiled, relief slowly starting to warm her.

Nellie had Watson snuggled up in a blanket like a baby. She passed him to Grace and said, "Here you are. I've dried him out as best I can, but he seems a little worse for wear."

"Watson, are you all right?" asked Grace.

He nodded slowly. "Mission rule eleven."

Grace frowned. "Wait, there is no rule eleven."

"There is now," Watson said. "No falling into floods."

Grace smiled and hugged him close. Watson might nag sometimes, but she loved him as a best friend, and she knew they had each other's backs.

She looked around for Tom. He was being patted on the back and congratulated by the villagers and Nellie. He glanced over, still looking concerned for Grace, but she gave him a big thumbs up and mouthed that she was fine and well done.

He smiled.

12

Watson's Raven School

The flood water disappeared swiftly, subsiding as the rain stopped, and everyone in the village was safe, thanks to Grace, Tom, Watson and Nellie. Frans milked Bessie the cow in the clockwork house, and Nellie made everyone warm milk and honey.

Grace's digi-com flashed and vibrated in her pocket. She quickly pulled it out and pressed the button. "Mum!"

"Oh, Grace, thank goodness," Mum replied. "Are you, Tom and Watson all right?"

"We're fine, Mum."

"Bren and I heard the dam near Brook Hollow had burst and we were frantic with worry. But the storm cut all communication, so I couldn't get through. We hoped you'd teleported home."

"We're still in Brook Hollow, but we're all fine," Grace said. "And so are the villagers."

"Thank goodness," said Mum. "It's so good to hear your voice."

Not far away, Bessie let out a happy moo.

"Grace, is that a cow I can hear?"

Grace laughed. "I'll explain later. Are you and Bren OK?"

"Yes, we're fine. There's been some bad flooding and storm damage, but we've helped lots of people and done our best. If you're all OK, we'll finish off here and head back to Copperport before dark."

"We will too. See you soon, Mum." Grace turned off the digi-com.

In the clockwork house, many words of thanks were being exchanged. The villagers could see how unfair they'd been to Nellie and were taking it in turns to say sorry.

"Thank you for saving my Bessie," said Frans. "I think she's grateful because I've never seen so much milk!"

"You nearly risked those poor wardens' lives for that cow," said Nellie, waggling her finger at Frans. "Well, I suppose I would have done the same for my ravens. We're not so different after all."

Frans thought for a moment. "I'm sorry for judging you wrongly," he said. "You'd be welcome to stay in Brook Hollow. There's space at the end of the village where you could put your house if you'd like?"

Nellie paused in thought, then said, "I appreciate the offer, but I'll be moving on. This has been my way of life for so long, it would be too hard to change it now. And I have my ravens to think about. But I'll stay around for a bit longer so you all have a safe warm space while you get your houses dried out."

Frans gave a nod. "If you ever want to visit in the future, even with the ravens, don't be a stranger."

"Thank you – I appreciate that." Nellie smiled and left Frans to walk over to Grace. "Speaking of ravens, I need to have a word with you and your robot friend. I've realised that this works both ways. Yes, the people of the villages aren't always welcoming to me, but I haven't exactly tried to stop my ravens from attacking people. I think I need a little help."

"What do you have in mind?" Grace asked.

"Perhaps a short lesson in raven behaviour before you go?" Nellie looked to Watson. "If you don't mind?"

Watson gave a salute with his wing. "It would be my great honour."

Grace tickled the cog under Watson's wing. "I like it," she said. "Raven behaviour school with Watson!"

Nellie and Tom laughed.

Grace looked to Nellie. "You'll always be welcome in Copperport, you know." Grace was thinking it would be nice to have Nellie around the city. Like an adopted grandmother. "Perhaps the city would suit you," Grace went on. "There are many people in Copperport who would appreciate your inventive brain, and you'd love the technology in the city. You could even open that mechanical toy shop you dreamed of."

Nellie smiled. "Ah, thank you, young Grace. But the mountains are my home now, and I'm not sure the ravens would like the city."

Grace gave a resigned nod and added, "If you ever need us, for anything, anytime, you just find a red box and call us. Even if only for a picnic with friends."

"Thank you, Grace," Nellie replied. "I should like that very much."

A few weeks later, back in Copperport, the sun was shining and the map was quiet. Mum declared that they were taking time off for a family picnic in Copperport Park.

"I'm so proud of you three and what you did in Brook Hollow. You saved a whole village from disaster," said Mum as she laid out the red checked blanket on the grass.

"It was all Grace," said Tom. "She thinks so fast when it comes to solving problems. I don't know what I would have done if she hadn't been there. I dithered at times and got scared when a house creaked a bit!"

"Hey, don't forget it was you that saved me with that mechanical bird in the end," Grace said, smiling.

Mum passed Bren, Grace and Tom a sandwich each and said, "Tom, none of us are perfect, and that's OK. It's our different skills that make us strong together. And we always have each other's backs because that's what families do. I know the more exciting part of our job is bringing down criminals and solving crimes, but perhaps the most important part is helping with the lower-profile incidents – the people who really need us. That takes a different strength. Your speech to the villagers was inspired from what Grace told me. Being tactful and understanding is often the best solution, rather than anger and force." Mum pulled Tom into a hug. "And you are full of kindness and understanding."

"What's that noise?" asked Grace, suddenly hearing a strange rhythmic clunking. She turned to the north end of the park and couldn't believe her eyes. There was Nellie's clockwork house strolling towards them.

"Ah! I hoped she'd make it," said Mum.

"You knew Nellie was coming?" asked Grace.

"I thought it would be a nice surprise. I guessed Nellie wouldn't have made it far from Brook Hollow, so I sent Watson on a secret errand."

Watson winked at Grace. "That mission your mum sent me on last week wasn't just to check on the Brook Hollow villagers."

"Who knew ravens could fib so well?" Grace said, and tickled Watson's chest.

Nellie reached them and called down from the steps above. "Hello, Griffins! I thought I'd take a trip to the big city after all!"

"Come down and join us!" Grace called up.

The ravens on the rooftop squawked happily.

"Whatever training you did with the ravens seems to have worked," Grace said to Watson.

Nellie joined them on the picnic blanket. "There's not a cloud in the sky, and I see we have lots of tea!"

Everyone chatted and laughed, and for once in a long time they weren't interrupted by another Moreland emergency. Although Mum still had her map sensor in her pocket – just in case.

Grace's heart filled with warmth. It was a perfect day: family, friends, sunshine and iced buns. Who could ask for more?

Our books are tested
for children and young people by
children and young people.

Thanks to everyone who consulted on
a manuscript for their time and effort in
helping us to make our books better
for our readers.

Don't miss Grace and Tom's next
exciting adventure in ...

The
WEATHERWELL

COMING SOON!